STAR HAWKS II

GIL KANE AND RON GOULART

tempo
books
GROSSET & DUNLAP
A Filmways Company
Publishers • New York

Star Hawks II
Copyright © 1978, 1981 by United Features Syndicate, Inc.
All rights reserved
ISBN: 0-448-17272-0
A Tempo Books Original
Tempo Books is registered in the U.S. Patent Office
Published simultaneously in Canada
Printed in the United States of America

First Ace Tempo Printing: July 1981

THE STAR HAWKS II TEAM

GIL KANE is the chief cover artist for Marvel Comics. He is a three time winner of the coveted National Cartoonist Society award for "Best Comic Book Cartoonist." During his more than 30 years as a professional comic artist, Kane has drawn virtually every major adventure strip character from Batman to Flash Gordon. Kane was the artist instrumental in the development of Marvel Comics and has worked on just about every book in the Marvel line.

RON GOULART is one of science fiction's most prolific writers. He has had 200 stories and articles published in magazines ranging from *Playboy* to *Ellery Queen*. Goulart wrote his first novel, "The Sword Swallower," in 1968. Since then, he has written about 100 more under his own name and several pen names. His most recent works are, "After Things Fell Apart" (Ace) and "The Eye of the Vulture" (Pyramid).

© 1978 by NEA, Inc.

THE *FLIGHT* WASN'T BAD...

...THE *LANDING* COULD HAVE BEEN A SHADE SMOOTHER.

SHORTED OUT, THE *ROBOT* PLUMMETS DOWNWARD...

KERBLANNNK!

RELAX... I KNOW A WAY OFF THIS BLASTED FLOOR.

WE'VE OVERCOME OUR FIRST CHALLENGE... BUT THERE'LL BE MORE!

YOUR *IMPROVISED* WEAPON WORKED.

YEAH, THOUGH I'D HAVE PREFERRED A LESS *DRAMATIC* FIELD TEST.

ALICEK...ARE YOU IN OKAY SHAPE?

YES, REX, I'M FINE...MORE OR LESS.

© 1978 by NEA INC.

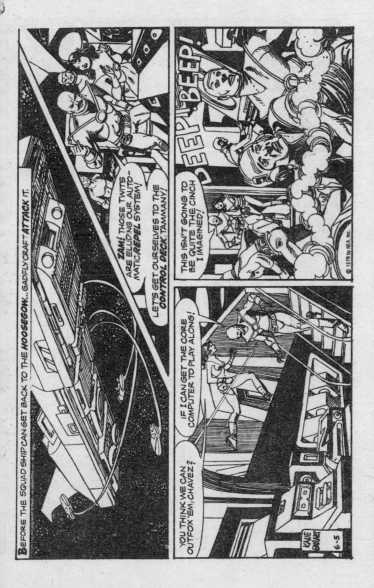

...REX AND ALICE K. ARE CONCERNED ONLY WITH EACH OTHER.

SO ON THE TROPICAL PARADISE FLOOR...

BUT THAT NEWS HASN'T REACHED THE HOTEL MAXIMUS YET.

AN ENORMOUS SPACE CRAFT HAS GRABBED CHAVEZ' SHIP AND... VANISHED.

KANE JOHN 6-15

© 1978 by NEA, INC.

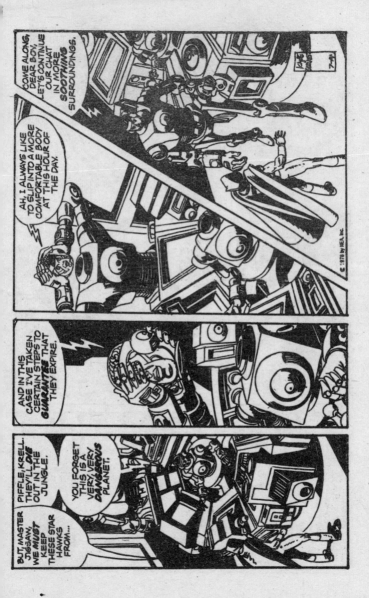

© 1978 by NEA, Inc.

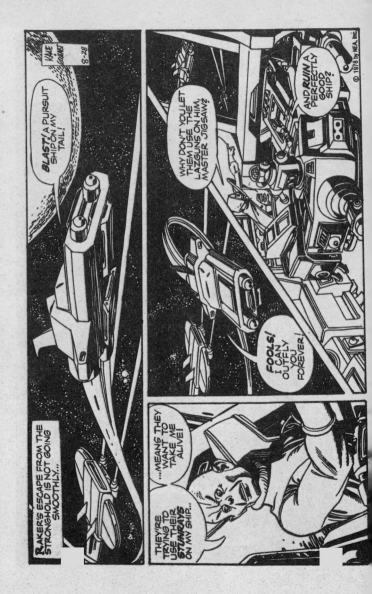